A New House
for Mouse

Introduction

One of the best ways you can help
your children learn and learn to read
is to share books with them. Here's why:

• They get to know the **sounds**, **rhythms** and **words**
used in the way we write. This is different from how we
talk, so hearing stories helps children learn how to read.

• They think about the **feelings** of the characters
in the book. This helps them as they go about
their own lives with other people.

• They think about the **ideas** in the book. This helps
them to understand the world.

• Sharing books and listening to what your children
say about them shows your children that you care
about them, you care about what they think
and who they are.

Michael Rosen

Michael Rosen
Writer and Poet
Children's Laureate (2007-9)

For Ralph

First published 2004 by Walker Books Ltd
87 Vauxhall Walk, London SE11 5HJ

This edition published 2011

2 4 6 8 10 9 7 5 3 1

© 2004 Petr Horáček

Concluding notes © CLPE 2011

The right of Petr Horáček to be identified as author/illustrator of this work
has been asserted by him in accordance with the Copyright, Designs and Patents Act 1988

This book has been typeset in Barmeno

Printed in China

British Library Cataloguing in Publication Data:
a catalogue record for this book is available from the British Library.

ISBN 978-1-4063-3505-7

www.walker.co.uk

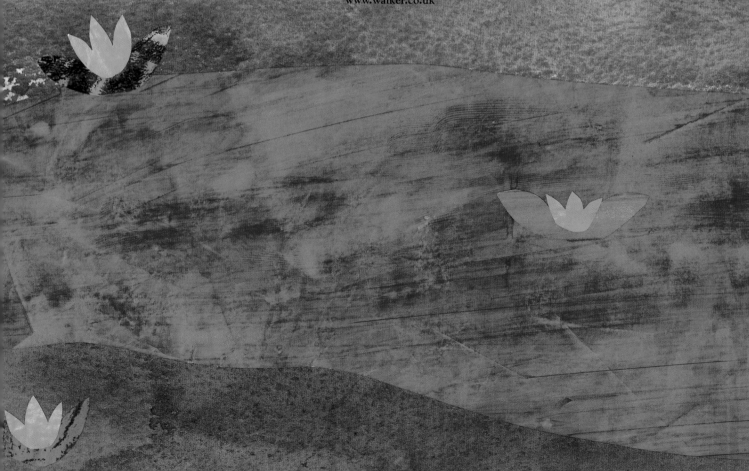

A New House for Mouse

Petr Horáček

WALKER BOOKS
AND SUBSIDIARIES
LONDON • BOSTON • SYDNEY • AUCKLAND

One day a little mouse looked out of the tiny hole where she lived and saw a huge apple.

"Goodness me," said Little Mouse. "I would like that apple to eat. I must bring it inside."

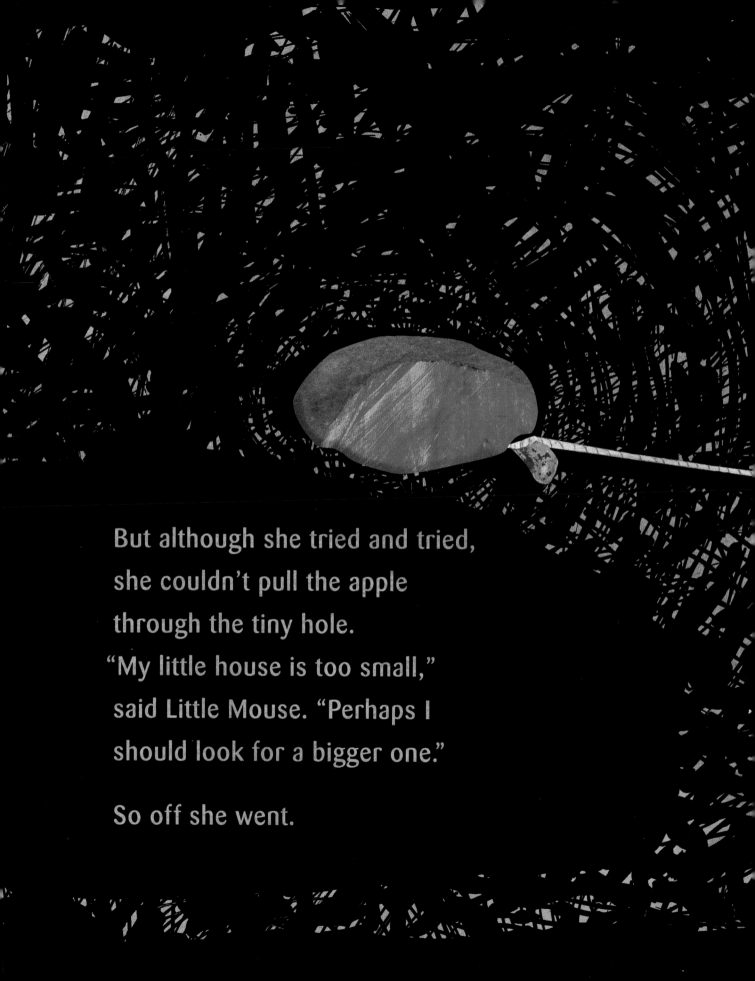

But although she tried and tried,
she couldn't pull the apple
through the tiny hole.
"My little house is too small,"
said Little Mouse. "Perhaps I
should look for a bigger one."

So off she went.

"Looking for a new house makes you hungry," said Little Mouse, as she took a few bites of the juicy apple. Then she spotted a hole that was a little bigger than hers. "This looks just right," she said as she peered inside.

"Hello, Mole," she said.
"I need a bigger house
for me and my apple.
Can I live here with you?"
"I'm sorry," mumbled Mole,
"but my home is too full
of books and I don't think
there's room for both of us."
"Perhaps not," said Little Mouse,
"I'll keep looking."

As she wandered, Little Mouse felt hungry.
"I'll just have a nibble," she said to herself.
Then she spotted a hole that was a little
bigger than Mole's. "That will be perfect,"
she said.

She peered inside.

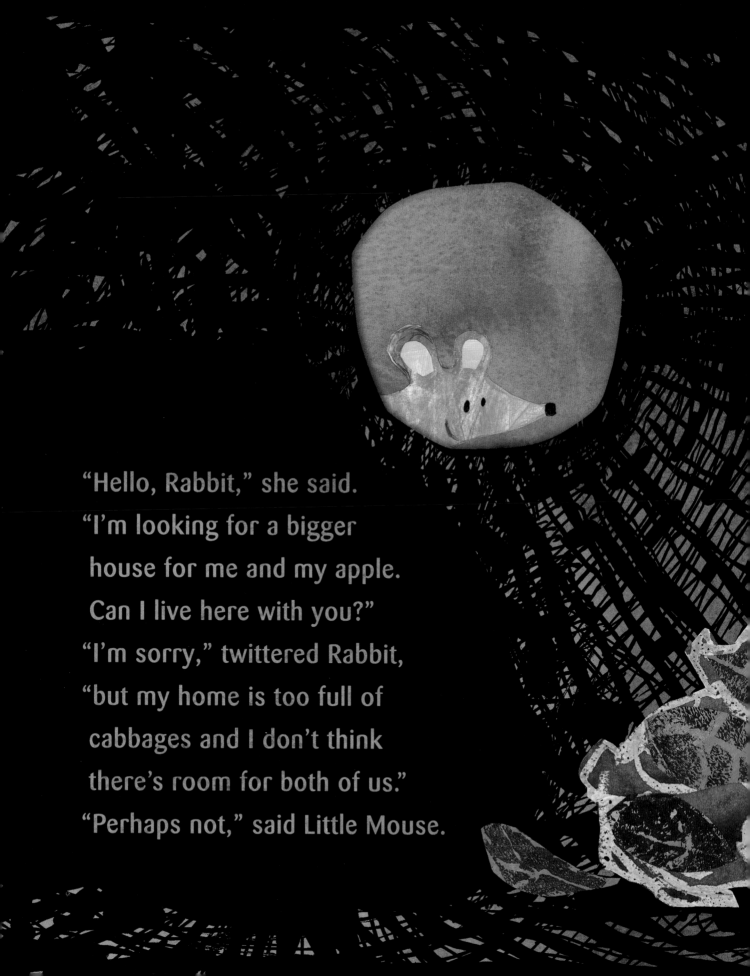

"Hello, Rabbit," she said.
"I'm looking for a bigger
house for me and my apple.
Can I live here with you?"
"I'm sorry," twittered Rabbit,
"but my home is too full of
cabbages and I don't think
there's room for both of us."
"Perhaps not," said Little Mouse.

She set off again, but she was
still hungry, so she nibbled on the apple
as she went. Then she spotted another hole
that was a little bigger than Rabbit's.
"That will be just right," she said.

She peered inside.

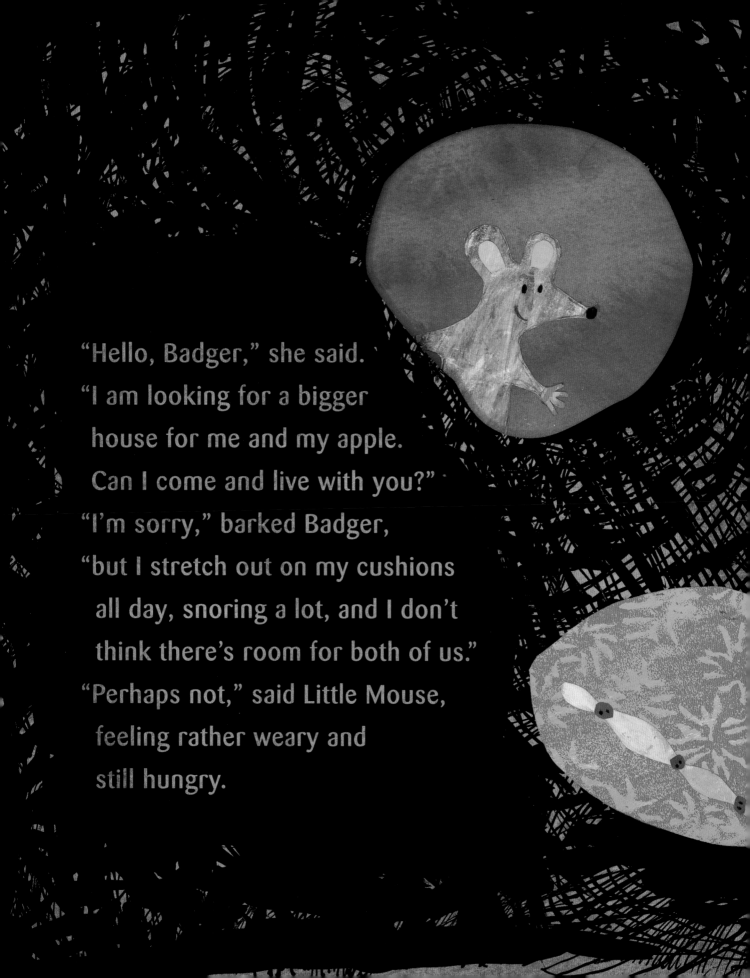

"Hello, Badger," she said.
"I am looking for a bigger
house for me and my apple.
Can I come and live with you?"
"I'm sorry," barked Badger,
"but I stretch out on my cushions
all day, snoring a lot, and I don't
think there's room for both of us."
"Perhaps not," said Little Mouse,
feeling rather weary and
still hungry.

That evening she came across an enormous hole. This must be big enough for me and my apple, she thought. **"Hello! Is anybody there?"** she shouted.

"Hello, little mouse," growled
a huge bear. "Why don't you
come and live here with me?"
"No, thank you," squeaked Little Mouse.
"I think the cave is a bit too small

for you and me AND

my apple."

And off she ran.

Little Mouse was tired now,
but pulling the apple seemed easier.
Suddenly she saw a tiny hole.
"That looks perfect," she squeaked.
"I wonder who lives here…"

She peered inside.

There was no one
at home. Little Mouse
went right in and pulled
her apple behind her.
It fitted perfectly.

"I knew I would find somewhere
just right for me and my apple,"
she said, and she climbed into her
own bed and fell fast asleep.

Sharing Stories

Sharing stories together is a pleasurable way to help children learn to read and enjoy books. Reading stories aloud and encouraging children to talk about the pictures and join in with parts of the story they know well are good ways to build their interest in books. They will want to share their favourite books again and again. This is an important part of becoming a successful reader.

A New House for Mouse is about a little mouse who is so determined to eat an enormous apple that she searches high and low for a house big enough to contain it until, at last, she finds the ideal home. Here are some ways you can share this book:

• As you read the story, invite children to guess who lives in each hole. And can they guess what happens in the end?

• The circular "shape" of this story (it ends where it begins) makes it a good one for children to draw like a map. They can add captions or labels to their pictures and use their map to tell the story out loud in their own words.

• This is a really good story to act out using different voices for each of the animals. Children can act it out themselves or use their toys to play the characters in the story.

• Using a shoebox, children can create a house for mouse, with an opening big enough for mouse but too small for an apple.

SHARE A STORY

A First Reading Programme
From Pre-school to School

Beginnings – 2 years+

Look Out, Suzy Goose · Walking Through the Jungle · Hello, Goodbye · Ten in the Bed · This Is the Bear · The Big Wide-Mouthed Frog

Early Steps – 3 years+

A New House for Mouse · The Train Ride · The Other Day I Met a Bear · Old MacDonald Had a Farm · The Tiger and the Jackal · Zed's Bread

Next Steps – 4 years+

The Hairy Toe · The True Story of Humpty Dumpty · Beans on Toast · Over in the Meadow · Dog Blue · Night-night, Knight And Other Poems

Taking Off – 5 years+

"Have You Seen the Crocodile?" · Handa's Surprise · The Ravenous Beast · One, Two, Flea! · Dinosaurs' Day Out · The Old Woman and the Red Pumpkin

Sharing the best books makes the best readers

WALKER BOOKS

www.walker.co.uk